The Roots of the dreams

Collection of Ethiopian short stories

Hithayadhulla

ISBN 978-93-5458-765-8
© Hithayadhulla 2021
Published in India 2021 by Pencil

A brand of
One Point Six Technologies Pvt. Ltd.
123, Building J2, Shram Seva Premises,
Wadala Truck Terminal, Wadala (E)
Mumbai 400037, Maharashtra, INDIA
E connect@thepencilapp.com
W www.thepencilapp.com

Author biography

The world calms down a bit by sharing some of the murmurs with literary interest.

A long time ago (remember 2001) I published a collection of short stories titled 'K. Ithayathulla' under the title 'Athanaiyum poyyaachu raasaa...('Everything is a lie my dear')' published by Manimegalai Pirasuram. Now I have the opportunity to write and publish it.

Although I was born and raised in my father's hometown of Nagapattinam, I have settled in my mother's hometown of Theni district in Chinnamanur.(South India).

CONTENTS

Preface

Athousand thoughts come to mind. There is not enough time to write.In the early 2000s and 2001, the Mig33 application even made it possible to chat on a button phone.Today social media has proliferated. The chat has seen a new evolution through telegrams today. Got some new friends.Some friends in Ethiopia especially mention my young friend Riham. She spends a lot of time with me. Lets share a lot of things. Lets get to know.So I wanted to translate Ethiopian's Amharic into English.

Iwould like to thank my Ethiopian friend Riham and friends and their telegram channels.Except I do this as an essence of literary work.There is no business purpose.See you in the next domain if the Lord wills.

by

Hithayadhulla

whatsApp:+918189941224

email:linuxhidhaya@gmail.com

Ethiopian's Short Stories

1.The Bricks!

When Will was young, his father owned a bakery. Outside the oven, there was a large wall. One day Will's father decided to look for a new wall in front of the bakery. He tore down the old wall and went to Will and his younger brother to build a new wall. At first, Will thought it was impossible.

There was no way he and his younger brother could build this wall. They thought that this place would be empty forever. But they started.

After school, they would go to the bakery every day and work on the walls. Every day they mixed concrete and laid bricks one at a time

 In time, the wall widened. A year and a half later, they put the last brick on the wall.

Will's father came out of the oven and all three stood in front of the finished wall. As he had planned, Will's father turned to them and said, "Don't tell me we can't do anything now," and they went back to the store.

"I learned that I did not set out to build a wall," says Will, who learned from that experience.

 You don't start by saying, 'I'm going to build the biggest and most amazing wall ever built.' They don't start there.

You say, 'I'll put this brick right, just like I put a brick.' 'If you do that every day, you will soon have a wall. " - Will Smith

Your life is the same.

 Don't go for less that your full potential. They don't start there, that's very unlikely. Have the ultimate goal in mind, but start by saying, "Today, I will lay my bricks as fully as I can." Your fitness, your business, your identity, your relationships, anything. Start by improving the first one and choosing the area of your life where you want to lay the first brick.

 If you are healthy, go to your first race. If so, read the first page of that book.

Whatever it is, make it small and accessible. Then lay another brick tomorrow. The next day another. If you do this every day, you will eventually have your own version. It only takes one brick a day.

When Will was young, his father owned a bakery. Outside the oven, there was a large wall. One day Will's father decided to look for a new wall in front of the bakery. He tore down the old wall and went to Will and his younger brother to build a new wall. At first, Will thought it was impossible.

There was no way he and his younger brother could build this wall. They thought that this place would be empty forever. But they started.

After school, they would go to the bakery every day and work on the walls. Every day they mixed concrete and laid bricks one at a time

In time, the wall widened. A year and a half later, they put the last brick on the wall.

Will's father came out of the oven and all three stood in front of the finished wall. As he had planned, Will's father turned to them and said,

"Don't tell me we can't do anything now," and they went back to the store.

"I learned that I did not set out to build a wall," says Will, who learned from that experience.

You don't start by saying, 'I'm going to build the biggest and most amazing wall ever built.' They don't start there. You say, 'I'll put this brick right, just like I put a brick.' 'If you do that every day, you will soon have a wall. " - Will Smith

Your life is the same.

Don't go for less that your full potential. They don't start there, that's very unlikely. Have the ultimate goal in mind, but start by saying, "Today, I will lay my bricks as fully as I can." Your fitness, your business, your identity, your relationships, anything. Start by improving the first one and choosing the area of your life where you want to lay the first brick.

If you are healthy, go to your first race. If so, read the first page of that book.

Whatever it is, make it small and accessible. Then lay another brick tomorrow. The next day another. If you do this every day, you will eventually have your own version. It only takes one brick a day.

2.Poor Horse!

Ayoung university student sits in the park with the professor's teacher

They talk. The teacher loves this student so much that he is like a friend to him

He took off his shoes in front of them and put on the park shoes

There is a maintenance worker, and the student looks at the cleaner

You and I are depressed, Why don't we trick anyone? The shoe he took off

We hid him and wondered how he would calm down when he lost his shoes

Let's see. "The teacher said:

We should not rejoice while suffering. If not, we have more money in our possession

We can find: Go and slowly put money on the shoes that the man took off

Come where you are: Then we will see what happens in secret. "The student cried as the teacher cried

The man's shoes came with a lot of money and he hid with the teacher

They began to monitor the man's condition. The man finished cleaning and put on his coat and shoes

He struggles to make ends meet, and when he bends over and takes off his shoes, he finds silver.

The man was shocked !! If he looks around, no one will see; And often looking right and left

No one. The man shook his head in surprise and put the money in his pocket

Later, when he set out on his second leg, he earned the same amount of money: the man

He did not believe !! He knelt on his knees and raised his head to the sky

You know that my wife is sick, but you know that no one can help her

No !! You saw my children's loneliness, didn't you !! Thank you, my lord. "

When the student looked at the man's condition, his eyes filled with tears

"I 'm sure you have more fun than you expected"

The student wiped away his tears and said, "Professor, if you have ever taught me this,

They never taught me, They taught me the most memorable lesson of my life;

Better a poor horse than no horse at all. "

3.Lucky Woman...

The son of a poor family loves the son of a very rich man, so

After spending a good time together in a neighborhood friendship, it ignites

Waiting for the day and time to express his love, he asks her for love: she

She replied, "What did you say ?! Let's be lovers ?!"

"If you understand, you are wrong

No, you are a miserable poor man

Destroying with my friends What are you going to put me through? Leave this idea alone and another

Find the right woman for you I can never love you like this "

The boy could not have hated her at all, but his heart went out to her just because she had pushed him

She's always been with him for 10 years

They meet the girl in: "How are you? Are you there? Still there

I married the best person who puts things in a car is smart on top of that

You know how much you earn per month if you have a higher salary of 15,000 birr

You still have a chance hahahaha ... "The boy said this ten years later

He wept again when he heard of the boy he loved again, as he wiped away his tears

The girl's husband came and said, "My lord has met my wife," and he turned to the girl.

"Surprisingly, this supermarket and millions of other capitals

He is the owner of the companies they own: I have not married yet: one

She was the girl he loved the most, but he won her heart with pure love

Unable to: What a good man you look like: a woman who has never met him

She must be a lucky woman blessed by the Creator of all things.

The girl remained dry

4.The Unseen

Question by question

One witness is being asked by a judge to testify in court

Judge: "Why are you here today?"

Witness "I testify that my neighbor was killed"

Judge: "Have you seen your neighbor killed?"

Witness "I didn't see it but I heard it scream"

Judge: "How can you speak only by hearing?"

The witness turned his face away and laughed

Judge: "What makes you laugh?"

Witness "Have you seen a laugh?"

Judge: "I have not seen but I have heard."

Witness "How can you speak only by hearing?"

5. Which book

The girl knocks on the door and opens it.

But because her father was so close, she did not greet him politely

Immediately coded so that the child would not be distracted

She: Hi, did you come to pick up your book "My Father is at Home"?

.

Son: Immediately he wakes up

The splendor of the festival

I was going to take the book "So Where Can I Wait for You?"

.

She: Oh, I didn't even get a book for him, but let me give you Yaadam Ratan's "Under the Shadow of the Mango Tree."

.

Son: Well, don't forget the book "I'll call as soon as I get there".

.

She: No problem

I also bring you the Ismael Gold "Come soon, wait for me" ....

As soon as the girl closed the door, her father stopped her

Father: Is it weird that he reads all this book?

.

She: Oh, Dad, you look so smart!

.

Father: That's nice. If so, I'll give you a book and take it.

.

She: Well, which book?

.

.

Father: There Hadis Alemayehu wrote on the shelf:

6.Important

One while a lawyer was traveling by train

A very beautiful girl came from the chair in front of her

She sat down. The lawyer was pleased. His eyes widened

They looked at each other and then she smiled. Now he is even happier. a few

She went and sat down next to him. This time he is very happy. a few

She paused and whispered in his ear, "Your money; your ATM card."

If you don't give me your nap ward and cell phone right now, you'll be dragging me

By telling everyone on this train that I was sexually harassed

I'm screaming. "The lawyer looked at her indifferently

He pulled out a piece of paper and a pen from his bag and wrote, "Sorry

I am deaf and hard of hearing. Please say whatever you want here

Write me on a piece of paper. "

The girl wrote down everything she had said before.

The lawyer took the paper and folded it nicely and put it in his pocket

It's good that he got up from his seat and said in a low voice, "Now

You can shout as much as you want. "

Behavior of the story: When is it important to keep a document properly?

7.Drunken

Aplane carrying many drunkards is on a flight;

The drunkards are shouting loudly and disturbing,

Meanwhile, a drunken pilot goes with him and argues that he should teach me how to fly

The pilot: It doesn't matter if you keep quiet about it

The drunkard goes to the drunkards and returns quietly.

The pilot was very surprised and asked, "What did you say to them?"

The drunkard opened the door of the plane and told them to go outside and play

25

8.Game of Thoughts

The child spent the first day working (as an assistant)

At night ... in his sleep, he cries out, "Piazza ... Piazza ... Piazza."

He woke his parents.

When the mother got out of bed and brushed her hair, she went to bed and slept soundly.

A little later he shouted, "Ambassador ... Ambassador ... Ambassador."

Once again, the mother sighs as she straightens her pillow and falls asleep.

5 minutes later, in a nightmare, he said, "Wollo Sefer ... Wollo Sefer ... Wollo Sefer."

They turned to their husbands and said, "What can I do?"

They say it's just a nightmare

Husband:

27

Stop it! "When the taxi fills up, it stops itself."

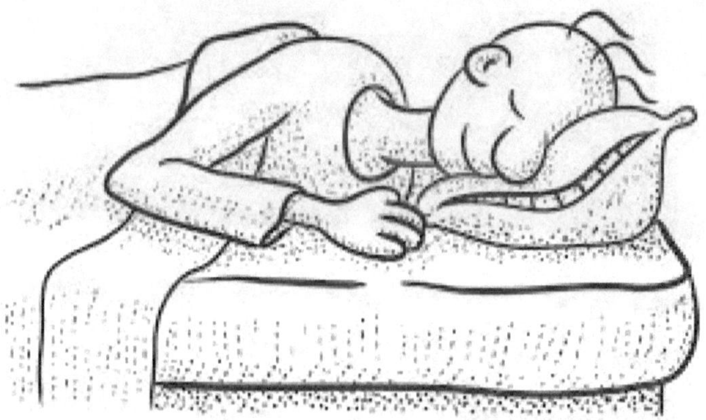

9.Happy

There was a girl playing in the park.

When she saw a picture in the forest, she put the photo in her pocket. But married.

She forgets the photo until she is.

Her husband asked, "Who is that little boy in your wallet?"

"My first love," she replied.

The husband smiled and said, "I lost this photo when I was nine years old."

10. Things

Wife (call)

Nonsense! Stupid! Where did you say that? -

Husband: I'm a piazza! -

Wife: What are you doing there ?!

Husband: Did you ever visit a gold mine?

Wife: I remember, my dear

Husband: When you see a gold bracelet, I like it.

Wife: Yes, my love.

Husband: Do you know the gold house?

Wife: Yes, my floor

Husband: I'm at the grocery store next to him

11. To gray

"Are you kidding me?" Elder Abba asked.

"Yes! He is. "She answered the question.

Tekalign came straight to her and kissed her on the cheek. Why does she only kiss on her cheeks?

He looked up and said, "Peace be upon you!" She did not respond to his greeting; She did not answer.

Yes! Why does she only kiss on her cheeks? Why did he only kiss her on the cheek, knowing her from childhood? She remembers being a child; One day, while they were exchanging orders, Titus took one of them to kiss him. He chose her. When she first kissed him, On her lips.

Since then, he has known her many times. She herself knows her name; Until he married another woman. She still sees him as he loves her, His eyes narrowed to see her. She can't deny that she loves him — especially his brown hair.

"How are you?" Mokshawa Halina, who followed Tekalni, kissed her again on the cheek. Mokshawa's conscience, which has snatched away her loved one.

She responded by giving him all her smiles; A smirk.

"All of you!"

When Mokshawa's conscience tried to greet the others, she turned her eyes away from me. He greeted all of them and walked to the blind man who was sitting on a high place. His legendary father, Abba Abate Tekalign, spoke to him before he reached them, as if he only knew that Kote was approaching.

"You said, 'Don't be late, my child.' A? Do you always have to revisit the story I started when you came !? "

It may seem that they are angry with each other. But she knew that Abba would never be angry with her. By the way, you never saw Dad get angry, From her childhood.

When Abba Tekalign approached them, they raised their hands. As usual, he put his head in their hands. They grabbed his ears, pulled him into their arms, and put him in their arms.

"Did he tell me who they were?" They asked him in a low voice, Looks like they don't want anyone to hear them. But their voices were heard.

Tekalni began to speak in a low voice, A voice that no one can hear except him. He spoke to them for a long time, and at some point the blind man's voice dropped.

"Didn't you tell me she was there in the first place?" "Conscience! ... Come here."

She knew that she was the one who had been called, so she got up and went straight to Abba Abba. I was replaced by Elder Abba.

When they came near to him, they lifted up their hands, and they did not touch him. She gave her head, She embraced them, Titus in front of her.

She looked up and saw the body in the elder's arms. But he was not watching. Struggling not to see her. Yes! He does not want his wife to yell at him when he comes home. She kept looking at Mokshawa to make him angry.

The old man hugged her and held her in his arms. As their hands came up to her head, I leaned closer to her, It's too close.

She would love to stay that way. But the hand of the father that came to cut her off was restored; He took my hand. Tekalign's face is red. Probably her red. Dad immediately began to talk to her.

"Why don't you come this season?" They asked.

"No! Dad was so sick that I could not get out of the house. "Everyone answered.

"Poor rain! He was a good man. Tell me, Lord, have mercy on me. " Father, an invisible movement.

Her father and father are old friends. Her father told her that they were friends even though they were in the army. But now both are old. Father, they have lost their light; Her father is healthy. In fact, it was Father Abba who first stopped moving; Because their eyes were blinded. From then on, they gathered the children of the village and told them stories they knew. But now there are no children. There were no children, but they did not listen; They listen.

She has seen many boring things in her life. Seeing Abba's gray-haired face; Even if they keep repeating themselves, But she never got tired of hearing their stories. Here it is: Then all the children grew up and started families; If this category does not include her. But they are still struggling to hear the legends they heard over and over again as a child. As a child, he would embrace them and embrace them.

Dad once pinched her and my ears and let them go. Tekalign hurried to walk in front of her and went to his wife. She went to her place.

As she sat on the floor, Father asked them all loudly. "What did I stop at?"

"When the man comes near you."

"Yes!" "Suddenly he came up to me and stopped. I looked at him in shock and said, 'Who will stand next to me in the midst of all this war?' "While I was watching ..." They repeated the word. "As I watched, his hair turned gray."

Father repeated the word. "As I watched, his hair turned gray."

Halina has heard this story many times through the mouth of the blind old man. But she still listens to them ... inspired.

"His clothes showed his chest. I saw his chest. You don't believe me ... "Abba still deliberately stopped talking. His chest hair is white. As I was preparing my sword, I saw Gion's logo on his shoulder, which had a chest strap on his chest, and I was relieved to learn that he was our man. What happened next was not what I expected. Then ... "They are still silent.

This is what you like from Abba Abate's narration: They know what to say or do to stop the story. And they do not remain silent for long. They continue to narrate only what they hear.

"Then it started to rise. At first, I thought that he was practicing magic. But it was not! The man was flying right. "

"No!" As they passed by, one of the passers-by, who had been waiting for the end of the story, saw that a legend was being told.

But he did not see the man. He was not waving like a bird. He was not jumping up and down. "They stopped as usual and continued. "that's it! It rises above the wall, as if it were carrying something. I can see it with my own eyes, which is exactly what it used to be. How can a person fly without telling the truth?

"When I left, I saw something I had never seen before. I thought he was just flying. But no! Many were flying side by side with him, Lots of gray haired people. When I saw that they were all our people, I felt more secure.

"They plundered the walls of Egypt like a light, and went down to the enemy. Later, the Egyptians opened the door for us and we entered. About 20 of them came in and opened the tower of the great pharaohs. I thanked the god because I could do nothing else; I thanked them for not being enemies with their gray hair. "

12. The Host

The couple goes to party at a restaurant

Often, when a couple goes to a restaurant, their game is more important than the food. After a while, they clap to invite the host

The host did not arrive .....

The applause still doesn't come ....

They clapped for the third time ...

Suddenly a funeral attendant came to them from the corner ...

Host: "What is applause? Are you at a wedding?"

"Come on ... my brother is obedient.".They are very shocked

Wife: "What if you had a hotel and hosted a World Cup like this?".

Host: "Just don't talk. Just say where you came from."

Wife: "Just what did you say?".

Host: "There's a crumb ... there's an egg crumb ... there's a fry ... there's a crumb again ... there's a fry again ...".

They are very angry"Just bring us some fries !!".

The host: "She'll come to you !!"

"You called me fried, didn't you?".

"Yes, it's fried."."Is it bread or bread?".

They are very angry and .."Bake us with bread".

He still doesn't order, he goes and comes back ...

"What should I bring for a drink?".

The husband says"Cocaine for her instead".

"She's coming. So what's the point?"

He still goes but comes back unharmed ...

"Is the soft inside out?".They are very angry and ...

"Let's just call the owner!".

"It's strange to call her husband!"

Still going and coming back ...

"Is the man the woman or the woman?"

13. The Guest

Aman, a lion, a donkey, a puff adder and an eagle were all going to war so they had to travel many days. As they were travelling one day, it became dark and they wanted somewhere to sleep. So they looked around and saw a hut with smoke coming out. So, following the trail of smoke, they went to the person's house. As was customary the travellers asked to spend the night.

But the husband and wife said, "We don't have any food to feed our guests, so what shall we do?"

They had a cow, so they thought about slaughtering the cow, but if they killed that, they would have nothing else.

So they talked it over with their guests, and said, "We have a cow, but that's all we have, and if we give it to you now, we expect to be repaid in the future. Tell us what you want to eat, and then tell us what you'd do for us in return."

So the lion said, "Can I drink the blood and maybe eat some of the cow as well, and I promise one day I'll repay you?"

And the dog said, "If I can have the bones, I will one day repay you."

And man said, "I want the milk and I also promise that one day I'll repay you."

And the puff adder said, "I want the nice white fat and I'll also repay you in a few years or so."

And the donkey said, "It's not actually the cow I want, but some nice grass from the thatched roof of your hut. So, if you give me some grass, I'll repay you."

And the eagle said, "Well, there's going to be some scrapings of meat on the leather hide. I want to eat that and I'll repay you too."

So the man and his wife slaughtered the cow and gave the lion the blood; the dog the bones; the puff adder the white fat; the eagle the meat on the hide; and the donkey some grass from the thatched roof.

So they went on their way.

The lion had said, "One day you'll hear me roar. And when you hear me roar come out of your hut, and you'll see what I will give you."

One day, early in the morning, the lion roared, and the man went out of his hut and found a huge ivory elephant tusk, and he was very happy and took it inside. Then he realised that there were no thieves around the whole area, and he discovered that the dog was guarding it, and he was very happy.

After seven years, the man's young brother, who was a very bad man, became rich. So the puff adder bit his brother and he died. According to the custom of the country, the man inherited all his brother's wealth, so he was happy.

Then the eagle one day saw that the elders were taking many valuable gifts to reconcile a husband and wife, who had quarrelled. So the eagle swept down and took away the valuable goods, and brought them to the man for him to use.

Only the donkey and the man were left.

Now, some people were using the donkey to transport silver that they laid on his back. As the donkey was going through the forest, he ran away suddenly and took the silver to the man.

But, surprisingly enough, the man never returned to keep his promise. He stayed away.

14. The Truth will...

The young man shouts loudly through the window of the train..." Dad Eyema the trees are following us!!!! ".....:

Father only smiles while watching his son.: The couple sitting in front of him shouting at the young man of 24 years old started watching him in the mood by drinking his lips. Still the youth are amazed and shouting....." Father Eyema clouds with us. He continued saying " ☞The couple couldn't keep quiet at this time and turned to their father's face..." Why don't you take your child to a good doctor..." After the father smiles...

" Yes, we were here we are now coming from the hospital. When he was a child, his eyes were missing, but today his eyes saw, that's why my child was wondering, he replied saying "

Everyone has his own history in this world. No matter if it's true, everyone has a reason for their own. Therefore, don't judge people by your own feelings and expectations because the truth will amaze you! or shock you! or it will hurt you!

I just wanted to say, everyone who is wise is not fool, but being silent is very wise.!:

Every single person on the planet has astory. Don't Judge people before you truly know them. The truth might surprise you

May God help us to have a wise and humble mouth!! Amen!!!

9 789354 587658